BENJAMIN AND THE SILVER GOBLET

To religious school teachers everywhere.
Thanks for your dedication. —J.J.

A story about brothers dedicated to my sister Samy. —N.U.

BENJAMIN AND THE SILVER GOBLET

by **Jacqueline Jules**   Illustrated by **Natascia Ugliano**

KAR-BEN
PUBLISHING

"You always leave me behind," Benjamin grumbled as he watched his brothers load their donkeys. "Let me go to Egypt with you."

"Father will not allow it," Reuben answered patiently.

"He treats me like a baby!" Benjamin objected.

But complaining was useless. Their father Jacob refused to let Benjamin travel.

"I've lost my favorite son Joseph," Jacob said. "I can't risk losing my youngest son, too."

So Benjamin stayed home and looked after the sheep. The grass was brown and withered. There was famine in the land and his brothers had left to find food.

"What is it like in Egypt?" Benjamin wondered. He closed his eyes and tried to imagine.

Every day, he climbed a hill to watch for his brothers' return. Finally, one afternoon, just as the sun was setting, Benjamin saw a figure in the distance.

"That's Reuben!" Benjamin recognized his oldest brother's curly black hair. Levi walked behind Reuben. Then came Judah, Issachar, Zebulon, Gad, Asher, Dan, and Naftali. But Simeon was missing.

"I'm sorry," Reuben told his father. "We had to leave Simeon behind."

"The governor accused us of being spies," Levi continued. "When we told him we had a younger brother and an old father at home, he didn't believe us."

"He said we had to prove we were telling the truth by bringing Benjamin to him," Asher added. "And he is holding Simeon in jail until we return."

Benjamin looked from one grim face to another.

Jacob put his hands on his heart. "Joseph is gone! Now Simeon is gone! How can I give up Benjamin, too?"

"I will take care of him." Judah knelt before their white-haired father. "I promise that your youngest son will be returned to you."

Benjamin held his breath, waiting for his father's answer. This was his chance to see the world.

"We have no choice," Jacob sighed.

Traveling with his brothers wasn't quite as much fun as
Benjamin had imagined. They teased him for being excited
about seeing new things each day.

"Look at our baby brother," Dan said. "His eyes are as
wide as the desert."

And at night, while Benjamin admired the stars, his brothers sat around the fire, complaining about the journey.
"My feet are sore," Gad moaned.
"I'm tired of dried meat," Asher declared.

Instead of listening to them whine, Benjamin often went to
his tent early. But one night, the conversation around the fire kept
him awake.

"It's our own fault," Reuben said. "We are being punished for
what we did to Joseph."

Benjamin sat up in his tent. What was Reuben saying? Benjamin
had been told that Joseph was attacked by a wild animal. His
brothers had brought back Joseph's blood-stained coat as proof.

"He was our little brother," Judah cried. "Why did we sell him as a slave?"

"Shhh!" Levi said. "You'll wake Benjamin! Do you want him to know what we did?"

After that night, Benjamin did not feel safe with his brothers. "They lied to Father about Joseph," he realized. "Will they sell me as a slave, too?"

A few days later, they arrived at a city bustling with people. Travelers from all over had come to buy food. The Egyptians had prepared for the famine, and their warehouses were filled with grain.

"Is that where the governor lives?" Benjamin asked, pointing to a palace in the middle of the city.

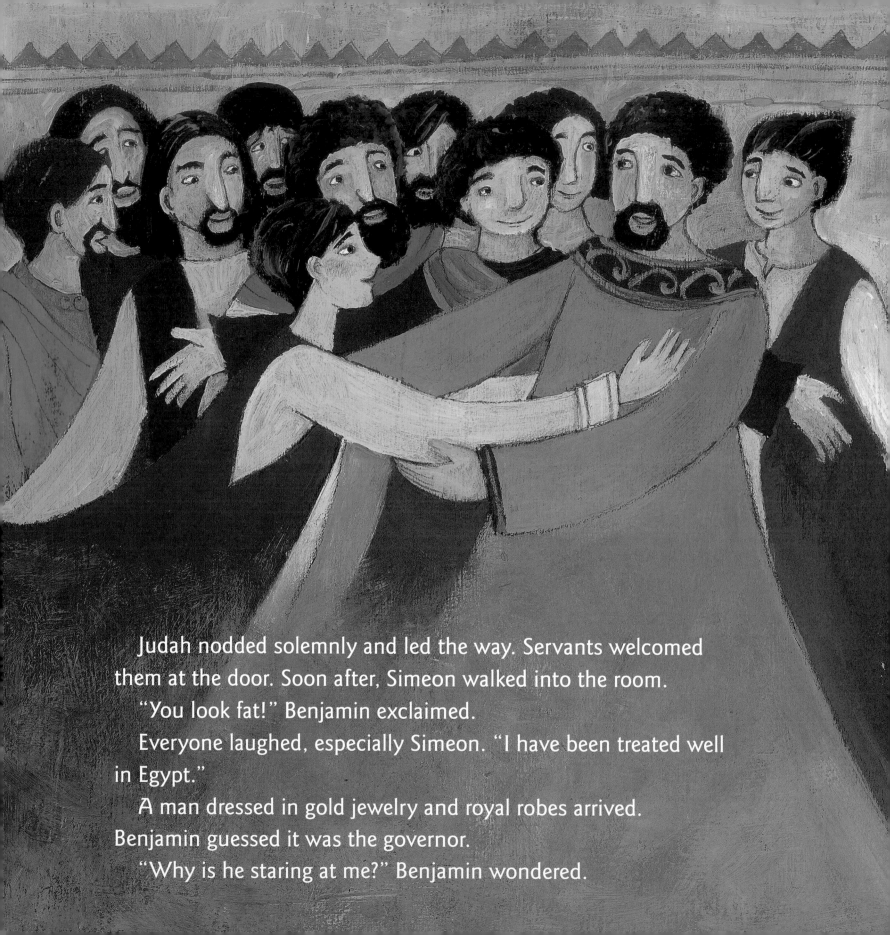

Judah nodded solemnly and led the way. Servants welcomed them at the door. Soon after, Simeon walked into the room.

"You look fat!" Benjamin exclaimed.

Everyone laughed, especially Simeon. "I have been treated well in Egypt."

A man dressed in gold jewelry and royal robes arrived. Benjamin guessed it was the governor.

"Why is he staring at me?" Benjamin wondered.

Judah took Benjamin's arm and stepped forward. "Here is our youngest brother."

The governor rubbed his eyes and turned away. "I'll be back in a moment," he said.

"Is there something wrong with his eyes?" Benjamin whispered to Judah.

Within minutes, the governor returned, clapping his hands. "Let us go to dinner."

The brothers were escorted to an elegant dining hall.
The governor amazed them by seating each brother at
the table according to his age.

"How does he know so much about us?" Benjamin
whispered to Naftali.

Naftali shrugged. "It is strange."

All evening, Benjamin sat beside the governor, eating delicious foods. The servants gave him double portions of everything.

Benjamin was uneasy. "Will my brothers notice that the Egyptian is treating me better?" he wondered. He remembered the day their father had given Joseph a colorful coat. His brothers had been jealous. Is that why they had sold him as a slave?

"What troubles you, young man?" the governor asked. "Does the food not please you?"

"The meal is wonderful," Benjamin said.

"Then enjoy!" The governor raised his silver goblet and smiled.

After dinner, he showed the brothers where they would sleep. "Tomorrow my servants will pack your bags with grain. Have a good journey."

At sunrise, they gathered their donkeys to return to Canaan. They had not traveled far when they heard the governor's servant calling. "Stop! Thief! Someone has stolen the governor's silver goblet. All bags must be searched."

Reuben, Simeon, Levi, Judah, Issachar, Zebulon, Gad, Asher, Dan, and Naftali lowered their bags. The servants found only corn. Then Benjamin lowered his bag. A servant pulled out a large silver cup.

Benjamin gasped. It was the same cup the governor had used at the banquet! How had it gotten into his bag?

"You are all under arrest!" the servant proclaimed.

The brothers were brought back to the palace where they bowed low before the governor. His angry voice echoed on the stone walls. "The one who stole my goblet will be my slave. The rest may go home."

Benjamin's stomach ached with fear. How could he prove his innocence?

"Please," Judah begged. "If I return
without my youngest brother, my father will
die from grief."

Benjamin raised his head. Was he hearing
right? Was Judah really defending him?

"Let Benjamin go with the others," Judah
said. "Take me instead."

These words made the governor turn his head away.
He wiped his eyes.

"Could he be crying?" Benjamin wondered.

"Servants," the governor ordered quietly, "leave me
alone with these men."

When the servants left, the governor motioned
with one ringed finger. "Come forward."
Benjamin stood in a line with his brothers.

"I am Joseph," the governor cried out, "the brother you sold into slavery."

They stared at the regal man. He wasn't at all like the boy they remembered from years ago.

"Do not be afraid," Joseph said. "I know now that you are sorry for what you did. I tested you, but you would not leave Benjamin behind. You would not hurt our family again." Joseph stepped down from the throne to embrace his brothers. They huddled in a circle and wept with joy.

They were again twelve brothers, united forever. And Benjamin knew he would always be safe with them.

AUTHOR'S NOTE:

For years, I have been fascinated by Joseph's test of the silver goblet. Would the older brothers abandon Benjamin in the same callous way they had sold Joseph years ago? Joseph created a similar situation to see what they would do. However, this time the brothers responded differently. They refused to return without Benjamin. This showed true remorse for their crime. In retelling this story from Benjamin's point of view, I had to imagine the feelings of a boy put at the center of a drama he did not quite understand. However, I stayed as faithful as I could to the plot of the story as translated in *Etz Hayim: Torah and Commentary* published by the Rabbinical Assembly of The United Synagogue of Conservative Judaism, 2001 and *The Torah: The Five Books of Moses* published by the Jewish Publication Society, 1962. For added details and flavor, I referred to *Legends of the Bible* by Louis Ginzberg published by The Jewish Publication Society, 1956 and *The Classic Tales* by Ellen Frankel published by Jason Aronson, 1993.

KAR-BEN PUBLISHING
A division of Lerner Publishing Group, Inc.
241 First Avenue North
Minneapolis, MN 55401 U.S.A.
1-800-4KARBEN

Website address: www.karben.com

Library of Congress Cataloging-in-Publication Data

Jules, Jacqueline, 1956–
    Benjamin and the silver goblet / by Jacqueline Jules ;
illustrated by Natascia Ugliano.
        p.   cm.
    ISBN 978–0–8225–8757–6 (lib. bdg. : alk. paper)
    1. Benjamin (Biblical figure)—Juvenile literature. 2. Bible stories, English—O.T. Genesis. I. Ugliano, Natascia.
II. Title.
BS580.B46J85 2009
222'.1109505—dc22   2007048344

Manufactured in the United States of America
1 2 3 4 5 6 7 – DP – 14 13 12 11 10 09